Little Otter's
Big Journey

For Tom - *D.B.*

For the handsome Monkey King - *S.W.*

Little Otter's Big Journey

Copyright © 2006 by Good Books, Intercourse, PA 17534
International Standard Book Number: 978-1-56148-548-2; 1-56148-548-9

Text copyright © David Bedford, 2006
Illustrations copyright © Susan Winter, 2006

Original edition published in paperback in the U.K. by Scholastic Ltd., 2006.

Printed in Singapore

Little Otter's Big Journey

David Bedford

Illustrated by Susan Winter

Good Books

Intercourse, PA 17534
800/762-7171
www.GoodBks.com

Little Otter was born on the edge of the big, blue sea.
He lay on his mother's belly, and he felt warm in the sun.
One day Little Otter's mother said, "I have to dive under
the sea to find food. Come with me and I will show you
how to do it."

Little Otter had never been under the big, blue sea before, and he was afraid. "I don't want to go," he said.
Little Otter's mother wrapped him in a blanket of seaweed. "This will keep you warm and safe until I come back," she said. "Wait here, and I will know where to find you." Then she slipped away under the water.

Little Otter waited. And he waited. It wasn't much fun being by himself.

He saw someone sitting nearby
on a post. Who was it?
He wriggled out of the seaweed
and floated over to find out.

"Little Otter!" said Pelican. "Why are you all alone?"
"My mommy is finding food for me," said Little Otter.
"I'm waiting for her to come back."
"But you are floating out to sea!" said Pelican.
"Wait here, and I will tell your mother where you are."

Flip! Flap! Pelican flew up and away, leaving
Little Otter alone again.

Little Otter waited and waited. It wasn't any fun being
by himself. Then he saw some animals waving to him.
Who were they? He kicked his feet and floated over
to find out.

"Little Otter!" barked the sea lions. "Why are you all alone?"
"My mommy is finding food for me," said Little Otter. "She'll
be back soon."
"But you are floating farther out to sea!" said the sea lions.
"Wait here, and we will show your mother where you are."

Plip! Plop! They dived under the sea, leaving Little Otter
alone again.

Little Otter waited while the sun went in and out of the clouds, and he waited while the waves started leaping and crashing higher and higher against the rock until . . .

. . . a giant wave washed him off, and Little Otter tumbled up and down, up and down, on the big, big sea. Little Otter was scared. Where was his mommy?

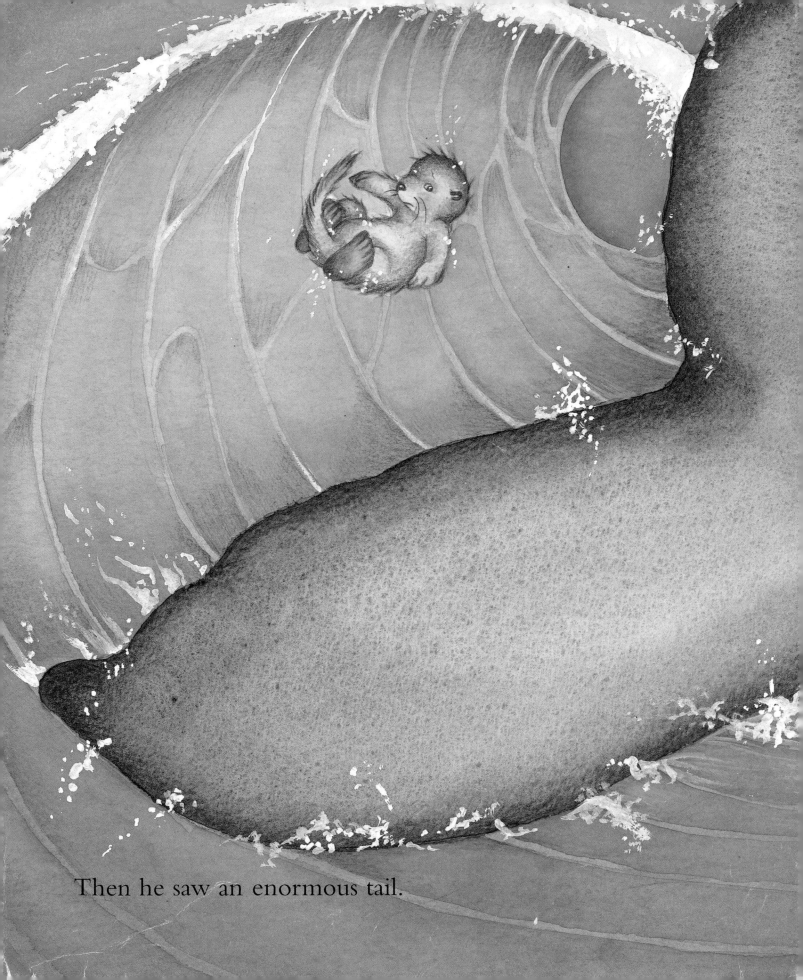

Then he saw an enormous tail.

"Little Otter!" said a kind, sing-song voice.
"Why are you all alone?"
"Whale!" called Little Otter with relief. "My mommy is
finding food for me, but I'm lost!"
"Hmm . . . ," said Whale, blowing a spray of water into the air.
"Wait here, and I will bring your mother to you."

Without a sound, Whale raised his tail and sank gently under, leaving Little Otter alone again.

Little Otter was cold and tired and shivery, and he didn't want to be by himself a moment longer.

He drew in a deep, deep breath, and shouted as loudly as he could . . .

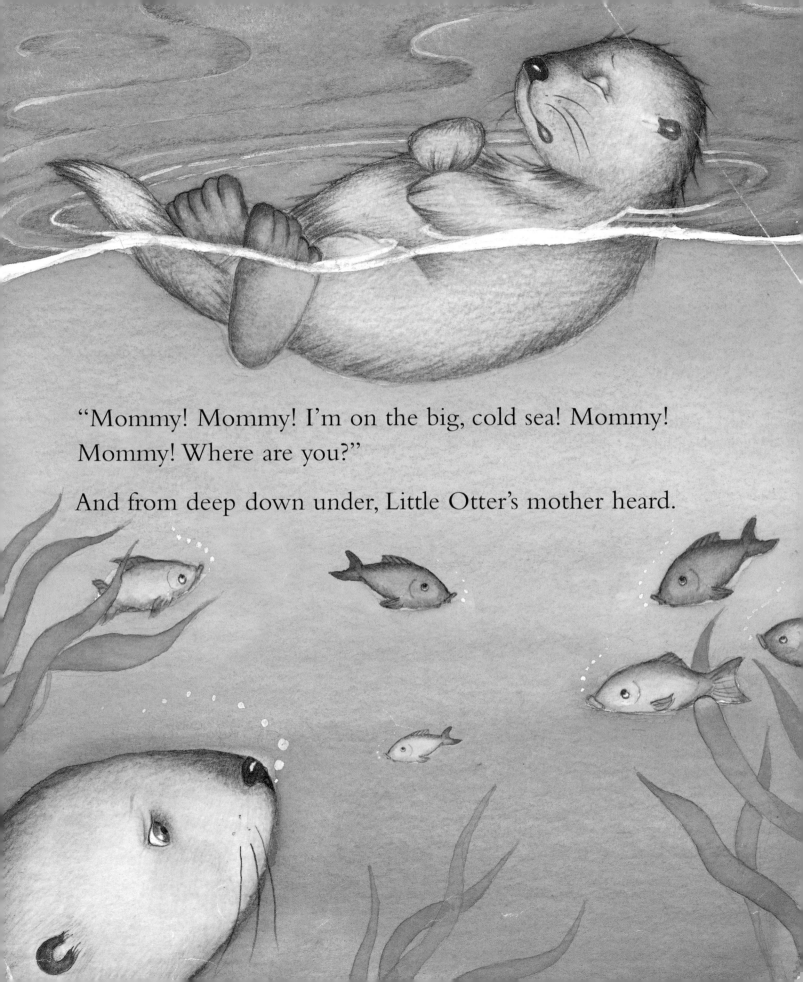

"Mommy! Mommy! I'm on the big, cold sea! Mommy! Mommy! Where are you?"

And from deep down under, Little Otter's mother heard.

"I'm here!" said Little Otter's mother.
Little Otter held on tightly as they bobbed about
on the waves.
"Never, ever float away, my baby," his mother said.
"I need to know where you are."
Little Otter shivered as a cold wave splashed him.

"We'll be warmer if we swim home under the sea," said his mother, soothingly. "And I will be with you."
Little Otter was still afraid to go under the big, blue sea, but he took another deep, deep breath, and when he dived with his mother . . .

. . . there were Whale, Pelican and the sea lions!
"My mommy found me!" Little Otter told them proudly.
"And now I'm swimming with her!"

When at last they reached their home, Little Otter said, "I'm going under the sea with you tomorrow, and the next day, and every day. And I'm never going to float away again."

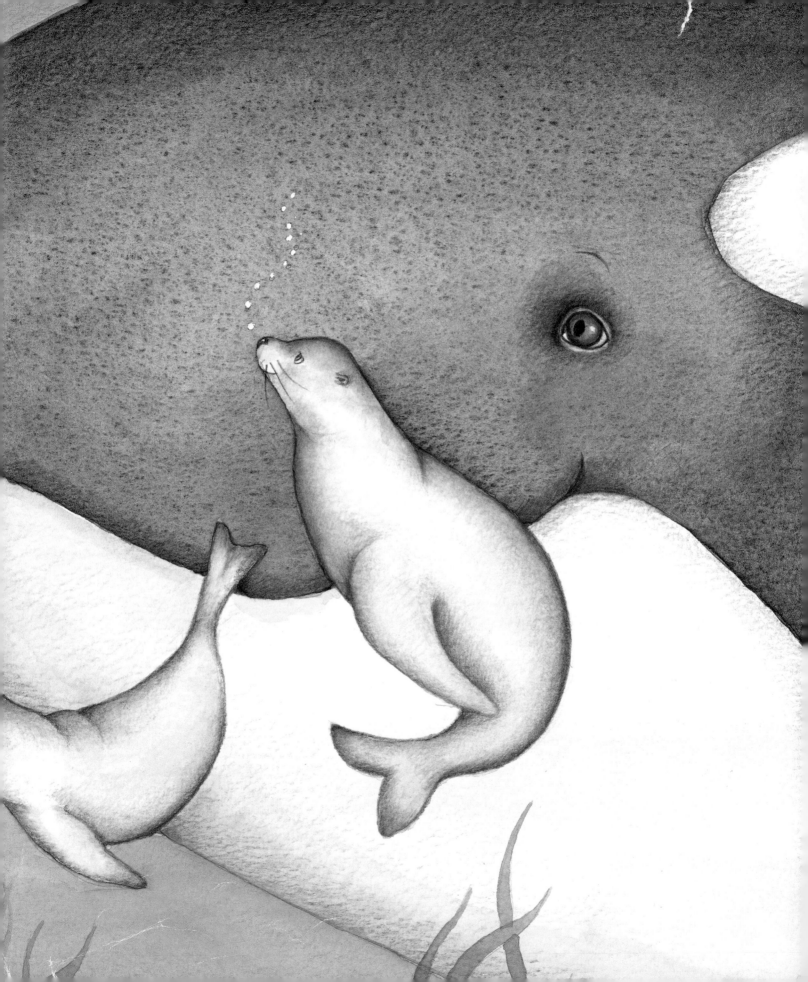

Little Otter's mother wrapped them both in a snug blanket
of seaweed, and as Little Otter fell gently to sleep, he heard
his mother whisper to him.
"No matter where you are, my baby, I'll always find you."